I dedicate this book to my two beautiful children.

-J.G.

Duncan and Daisy

"Guess what!...We're moving!"

Written & Illustrated by Joy Garcia

Over here are some pictures of Mommy and Daddy.

Daddy works for the military; that's why he's wearing that uniform.

What kind of home do you think
Duncan and Daisy will have?

Meet the real Duncan and Daisy.

More Duncan and Daisy books:

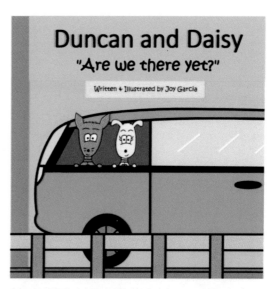

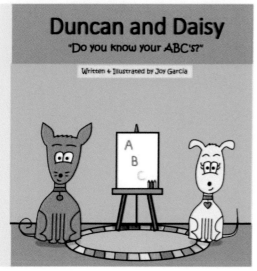

Made in the USA
Middletown, DE
15 March 2021